ella
the enchanted princess

Who Are You?

Written and Illustrated by
Rosaria L. Calafati

Follow Ella The Enchanted Princess at:
www.ellatheenchantedprincess.com

Books and E Books may be purchased at:
Amazon.com

Because of the dynamic nature of the Internet, any web addresses or links contained in this book may have changed since publication and may no longer be valid.

Print information available on the last page.

ISBN: 9781549756061 (sc)

Imprint: Independently published

Date Published: 10/21/2017

This book is dedicated to

my beautiful
daughter Helen

To my beautiful daughter Helen, you are the "Wind Beneath My Wings"!
Thank you for your support and inspiration. You are my true Princess Ella...
the little girl that always said "I Can't" and now is an "I Can" lady. You
supported me throughout my ups and downs and believed in me so I
could write and illustrate this book. You are amazing!

Love you,
Mommy

Here is the story that takes place in a beautiful kingdom hidden beyond the Enchanted Forest called Faylin.
This town was not an ordinary place, but a grand place filled with mysteries and wonder.

Deep in the Enchanted Forest
was a quaint castle that stood
all alone. Everything about
this place was mystical and
magical! In this castle, nestled
in the snow-covered mountains
surrounded by a moat, is
where this story begins.

FAYLIN

A very special little girl lived in this castle. Her name was Princess Ella. She was a beautiful princess with big purple-blue eyes and pink heart-shaped lips! She wasn't any ordinary princess; she was unique and amazingly brave!

Princess Ella had a big room where she spent all of her time. In her room, she had everything all little girls dream of having. She had wonderful toys, lots of books and a lot of costumes to play make-believe, which was her favorite thing to do!

Ella likes to pretend she lives in her happy dreams. In her dreams, she is not afraid of anything especially mirrors!

She doesn't like looking into mirrors. She is always afraid of what she might see. She knows that in a mirror, you see your exact physical reflection and she never liked what she saw!

The only mirror she wanted was the mirror in her room, Molly Mirror. Molly sat on top of her vanity next to Ella's beautiful crown, which she never wore. Molly Mirror is Ella's best friend. Ella always asked Molly many questions, and she knew Molly would always tell her the truth.

Ella never roamed around the castle because to get to any of the rooms in the castle; you had to go through the Grand Hall.

In the Grand Hall were mirrors. There were all kinds of mirrors big mirrors, little mirrors, round mirrors, skinny mirrors and more fancy mirrors.

These mirrors were the guardians of the castle. They only allowed people they recognized to roam the castle.

All the mirrors were very magical. When you walked by them, they spoke to you! Ella was so afraid to walk by them, for she always worried that they would tell her that she wasn't beautiful.

Every day, Ella would wait for Nanny to come to her room and read to her. She loved getting dressed up and pretending she was the character in the story that Nanny read. Nanny read very magical stories. There were stories about princesses in kingdoms all over the world, mermaids and even Cowboys and Indians. Ella loved stories about magic carpet rides, spells and potions and even scary stories about witches and goblins.

Ella was so happy when she pretended to be a character in these stories. Her favorite was being a mighty dragon slayer or even a pirate on a treasure hunt. How fantastic to play in a magical land and dance with the trolls and fairies and not having to worry about looking into mirrors.

Ella kept all her costumes in a large armoire that stood next to Molly Mirror. She had all kinds of hats, scarves, bandanas, and headbands. Her beautiful princess dresses were in the armoire too, but Princess Ella didn't even look at them.

She would wait for Nanny to read to her to get dressed in character for the day. She always made sure to wear something on her head. When she wore something on her head, it made her feel beautiful!

Another place that Princess Ella dreamed of going was the Enchanted Forest. She heard so many stories about the Enchanted Forest that were exciting. She always wondered if it was magical like the stories she loved reading.

Nanny told stories about an Ogre named Bullock, who lived in the Dark Forest. What would Ella do if she ever met him?

"Only if I wasn't so afraid of the mirrors," she thought, "I would be able to go outside and explore the Enchanted Forest."

Ella loved hearing her stories and loved her books. She was very curious and wanted to know where she could find all these books! One night when Nanny was tucking Ella in, she asked Nanny, "Where do you get these amazing books?"

Nanny looked at Ella and told her, "Down the hall behind the massive wooden doors!" Ella became very curious about the wooden doors!

Nanny said, "One day, Ella, when you are ready, you will go down the Grand Hall and see for yourself what's behind those doors." What did Nanny mean when she said when I was ready?

Every day, Ella thought she was ready to leave her room. She opened the door and stepped out of her bedroom and looked down the steps, past the hall, to get a glimpse of those two intriguing doors. Ella knew they had to lead to someplace beautiful.

I want to go behind the wooden doors, she thought, but the thought of walking past the mirrors always made her stop. Then she would sigh and go back to her room and close the door behind her.

Ella was so curious about the majestic doors that one morning, Ella shouted out, "Today is the day!" She looked at Molly and said, "Today is going to be a magical day!" She told Molly Mirror she was going to go down the Grand Hall to the Majestic Doors!

"I know I am ready to face the mirrors!" Ella said to Molly. "I will wear my boa and my fluffy purple hat to explore the hall." All dressed up with her hat on her head; she told Molly Mirror, "I am ready!" Molly just rolled her eyes.

I will open the door, take a deep breath and walk outside. I will make sure I hold my head high. "There is nothing to be afraid of, right Molly?" Molly smiled and agreed, and off Ella went to the Grand Hall.

As she began walking down the Grand Hall, the Big Mirror stopped her and asked, "Who Are You?" Princess Ella frowned and said, "It's me, Princess Ella." "Oh no, you're not. You don't look like Princess Ella. Go back; you are not allowed in these halls," shouted Big Mirror.

Princess Ella was so confused to hear what Big Mirror said. She ran back to her room and took off her hat and boa and sat on her bed. She was very upset. "What happened, Ella?" asked Molly.

She gave Molly a weird look. Ella said, "The Big Mirror said I wasn't Princess Ella! What did he mean by that?" She wondered why Molly Mirror recognized her and not the Big Mirror. What was going on?

Ella was ready to try again, "I know, I will look for something more beautiful and a bigger headband to put on my head." Molly Mirror just sighed.

Ella found a beautiful ballerina gown costume with lots of ruffles and sparkles and a beautiful floral wreath headband. "This is bigger and prettier to wear!" Ella told Molly. Ella thought she would look exquisite and the mirrors would surely know who she was!

This time, she crawled past the Big Mirror who looked like he was ready to fall asleep. She was so happy that he couldn't see her. She was getting closer to the doors when all of sudden, she heard a little voice. "I know you think I don't see you," said Little Mirror. "Who Are You?"

Ella was so surprised to hear this little voice. She thought she escaped being seen by Big Mirror. Ella said, "I am Princess Ella." "Oh no you're not, you're not Princess Ella" replied Little Mirror. "Please leave the hall." Now Ella was in tears as she ran back to her room.

She threw her headband on the floor and started to cry. Molly Mirror said, "Please don't cry, Ella. You are making me sad." Ella thought for sure she was ready to go down the halls. What went wrong?

What should she do to get by the mirrors in the hall? "It's useless trying to get passed the mirrors in the room. They don't even know who I am. I will never see what is behind those majestic doors." she said to Molly.

Feeling somber, Ella went over to her vanity and sat down. She looked at Molly and said, "Why do you know me, but the mirrors in the hall don't even recognize me?"

Molly took a deep breath and said to Ella, "Maybe it is because I see how beautiful you are. You don't need to put those silly things on your head. You are beautiful just the way you are.

You don't have to wear a costume or pretend that you are anyone else but YOU!" Ella was so surprised at what Molly was saying, and she knew that Molly was telling her the truth. Could it be that simple? After thinking about what Molly said, Ella replied, "Really, Molly? I just have to be me, Princess Ella!"

"Now it is time to go out there and show them who you are," said Molly Mirror. With Molly's help, Ella put on her beautiful princess dress and her beautiful princess shoes. She looked at her beautiful princess crown and wondered if she was ready to wear it. All of sudden her crown started to sparkle as if it was trying to tell Ella something.

Then the room filled with pink sparkles and her crown floated up high in the air, right above Ella's head. She looked up at the crown and nodded yes, she took a deep breath as the crown softly landed on her head. She looked at Molly and then smiled and said, "Thank you for telling me to believe in myself!"

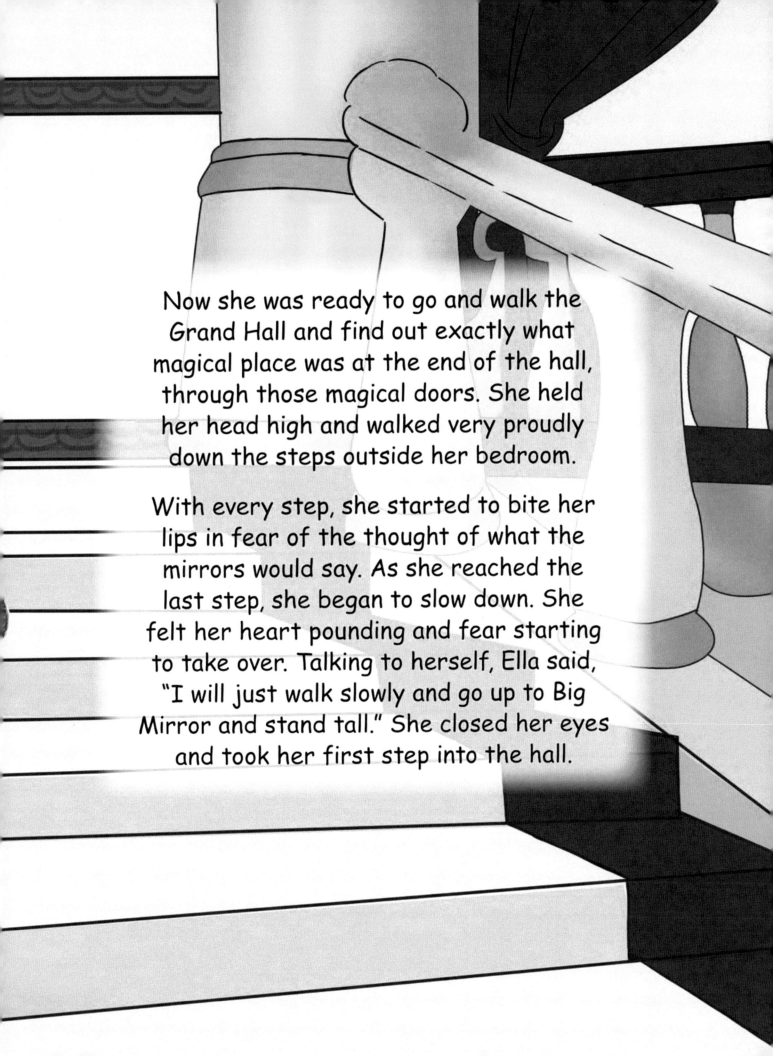

Now she was ready to go and walk the Grand Hall and find out exactly what magical place was at the end of the hall, through those magical doors. She held her head high and walked very proudly down the steps outside her bedroom.

With every step, she started to bite her lips in fear of the thought of what the mirrors would say. As she reached the last step, she began to slow down. She felt her heart pounding and fear starting to take over. Talking to herself, Ella said, "I will just walk slowly and go up to Big Mirror and stand tall." She closed her eyes and took her first step into the hall.

All of a sudden, she heard a big voice, "There you are my beautiful Princess Ella. Good morning to you!" Ella could not believe her ears!

As Princess Ella looked around, she saw the reflection of a beautiful princess in all the mirrors of the Grand Hall. She was victorious when she realized it was her reflection that was in the mirror! As Ella walked down the hall, every mirror said good morning and knew who she was! Ella learned that being herself is all it took!

Finally, she was at the beautiful, magical doors. Overcome with excitement, Ella opened the doors and stepped inside. To Ella's surprise, Nanny was standing right there! She greeted Ella and said, "I am so proud of you, beautiful Princess Ella!"

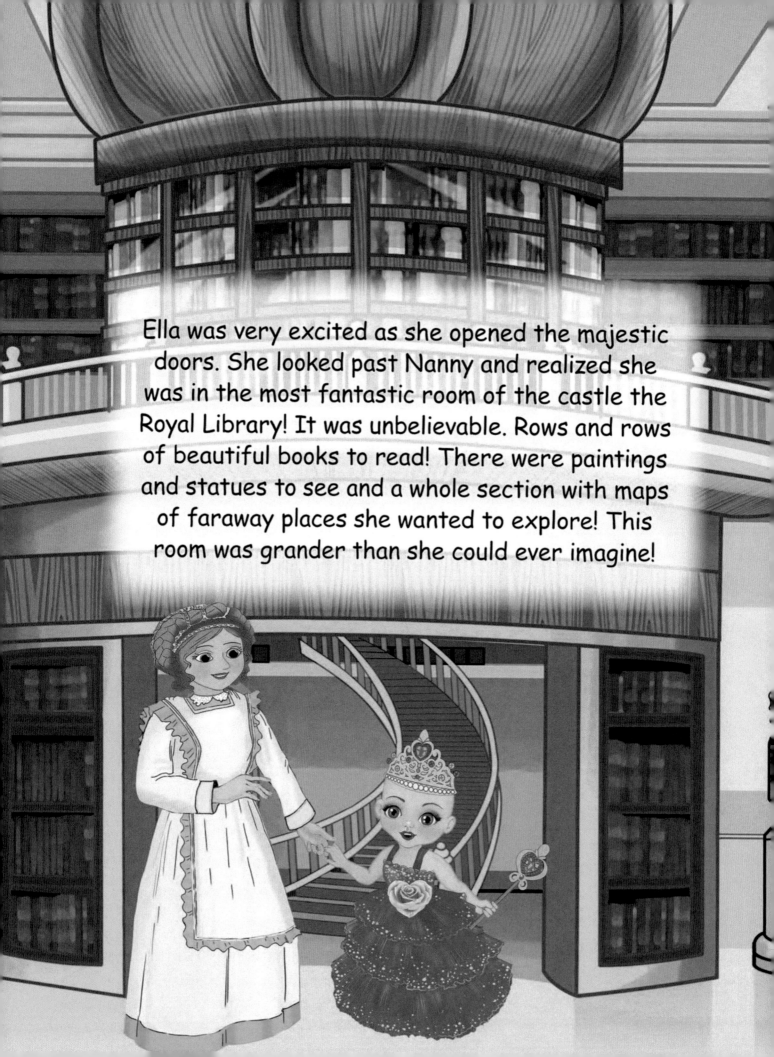

Ella was very excited as she opened the majestic doors. She looked past Nanny and realized she was in the most fantastic room of the castle the Royal Library! It was unbelievable. Rows and rows of beautiful books to read! There were paintings and statues to see and a whole section with maps of faraway places she wanted to explore! This room was grander than she could ever imagine!

She took Nanny's hand and said "Where do I begin? These books will take me on so many new adventures! I can't wait for you to read to me so I can start my new journeys!"

Princess Ella became friends with the mirrors in the Grand Hall. Every time the mirrors saw her, they told her that she looked beautiful and they let her go wherever she wanted to go!

Ella starts exploring the castle and ventures into the Enchanted Forest. She enjoys going to the garden and singing to the birds and butterflies! What an amazing feeling not being afraid anymore! She loved staying in the courtyard and daydreaming of more adventures that she may face.

Ella will always read her amazing stories and dream of taking many adventures. She wonders if her enchanted dreams will ever come true. Ella's imagination is so big that Ella doesn't know where to begin. Why not join Ella as she takes many adventures to help protect the Enchanted Forest?

Follow Ella as The Enchanted Princess goes on a dangerous quest to find a magical purple gem that saves the fairies and their home. Be with her as she meets the trolls to locate the light of the Enchanted Forest. Are they as scary as everyone says?

Ella's biggest fear is of Ogre Bullock. Help her try to avoid Ogre Bullock as he tries desperately to swallow her imagination. Will he succeed in making the Enchanted Forest disappear as he takes the color out of everything around him? Will Ella ever convince Ogre Bullock to become her friend or does she have to learn how to stop him?

About the Author

Rosaria L. Calafati is a very devoted wife, mother, and grandmother. Her family means the world to her. She has six grown children and 11 grandchildren! She also has a marvelous husband who has inspired her throughout her challenges of Breast Cancer.

She has a unique imagination and loves to use it to make her family happy. Her biggest asset is her imagination to create wonderful holidays, parties, and activities to keep her family entertained and always believing in themselves. Her whole life was all about children and giving them a positive way of facing their deepest challenges.

Being a Breast Cancer survivor and a devoted mother inspired her to create Princess Ella. Going through the many difficulties of Breast Cancer, losing her hair was the one thing that changed her way of looking at life. She wrote this book to inspire children and teach them that they are very beautiful in their own special way! People are beautiful just the way they are. Children have a special place in her heart, and through her books, she hopes to teach children to believe in themselves!

Made in the USA
Coppell, TX
06 November 2020